LOWRIDERS in SPACE

By CATHY CAMPER
Illustrated by RAÚL THE THIRD

chronicle books·san francisco

ELIRIO MALARIA, FLAPJACK
OCTOPUS, AND LUPE IMPALA
LIKED WORKING WITH CARS.
THAT WAS THEIR JOB.

12

ELIRIO MALARIA

ELIRIO WAS THE BEST DETAIL ARTIST AROUND. PEOPLE WERE A LITTLE AFRAID OF ELIRIO MALARIA.

Don't be scared, eses!* Only lady mosquitos bite vatos for food!

WITH A BEAK LIKE THAT, THEY THOUGHT HE MIGHT BITE.

* BUDDIES, DUDES

* AND THERE'S A TON OF CARS!

THEY ALSO DREAMED OF HAVING THEIR OWN CAR.

THEY'D SEEN SOME CARS BLAST BY FAST . . .

. . . AND OTHERS THAT COULD SHIFT AND DRIFT . . .

21

UNIVERSAL CAR COMPETITION

New Cars, Race Cars, Funny Cars, Scrapers, Dragsters, Art Cars, Donks, Stock Cars, Hot Rods, Muscle Cars, Collectibles, Demolition Derby Cars, Convertibles, Station Wagons, Coupes, and Sedans. — All Ranflas* Accepted

THE MOST MECHANICALLY INVENTIVE, EXQUISITELY DETAILED COSMIC CAR WINS!

$$ **First-place prize:** A carload of cash and a solid gold steering wheel.

* LOWRIDERS

THEY HAD THE START OF A CAR, THE SHELL OF A CAR. IT WAS ALREADY LOW AND SLOW. SO SLOW, IT DIDN'T EVEN GO.

* AND WE WILL HAVE TO GIVE IT OUR BEST!

* MONEY

31

BY THE TIME THEY REACHED THE STRATOSPHERE, THEIR CAR WAS GOING . . .

. . . LOW AND SLOW, BAJITO Y SUAVECITO.

* GIVE IT SOME GAS!

** A DANCE FROM COLOMBIA *** COOL!

43

Red planet straight ahead.

WHEN THEY LANDED ON MARS, FLAPPY FELL IN LOVE WITH THE CRIMSON LANDSCAPE.

Oooo, just like the beach!

HE COVERED THE SEATS IN RED SAND VELVET . . .

That's smooth, Chavo!

. . . TURNING HILLS AND VALLEYS INTO PERFECT TUCK AND ROLL.

TO FLAME UP THE EXHAUST, LUPE POKED COMET TAILS UP THE TAILPIPE.

FLAPJACK CAUGHT FLYING METEORS FOR BLAZING HEADLIGHTS.

AND THEY NICKED THE FORMER PLANET PLUTO FOR THEIR GEARSHIFT KNOB.

LUPE CLIMBED INTO THE DRIVER'S SEAT AND TURNED THE KEY.

Add some dust from la luna de conejo* and our car will *really* hop!

Start her up!

ELIRIO FLIPPED THE SWITCH TO GET HER GOING.

Light, heavy.

Heavy, light.

It dips!

* THE RABBIT IN THE MOON. (IN THE UNITED STATES, PEOPLE SEE A MAN IN THE MOON, BUT AZTEC CULTURE SAW A RABBIT IN THE MOON.)

AS A FINISHING TOUCH, ELIRIO WRANGLED A FEW RINGS AWAY FROM SATURN . . .

I think we're done!

* JUST AS YOU BEGIN A STORY, "ONCE UPON A TIME...," THESE ARE NONSENSE WORDS THAT MEAN IT IS THE END OF THE STORY.

* THICK MEXICAN SAUCE FOR MEAT MADE OF MANY INGREDIENTS, INCLUDING PEPPERS AND CHOCOLATE

THE UNIVERSAL CAR COMPETITION HAD ALREADY BEGUN.

So many cool cars!

Judges, are you ready to make your marks?

VROOM!

THE JUDGES LOOKED AT CARS THAT BLASTED BY FAST.

CARS THAT SHIFTED AND DRIFTED,

AND CARS THAT WERE LOW AND SLOW.

EVERY PART OF IT WAS FIXED AND PAINTED, SHINY, RECOVERED, AND REDISCOVERED.

* OLD AND NEW

LOWRIDERS in SPACE!

Lupe Impala!
Elirio Malaria!!
El Chavo Flapjack!!!

Yours is truly a universal car,

THE most mechanically inventive, exquisitely detailed car in the universe!

A NOTE ABOUT LOWRIDERS

Lowriders were created by Mexican Americans, and originated in Southern California after World War II. The first customized cars were street racers and hot rods, built by Anglos and Mexican Americans alike. Both groups thought their cars looked cooler when they were modified to ride lower to the ground.

Anglos continued to build hot rods while Mexican Americans developed their own vehicles that rode low and slow, which made them good for cruising neighborhood streets and hanging out with friends and family. And of course, both groups used their cars for flirting and for competing over who could build the best car.

Many Mexican Americans couldn't afford new cars, so they modified old ones to create cars that drew respect. They often chose Chevys over Fords because Chevys were readily available and were considered more reliable and better-looking. The Chevy Impala remains a lowrider favorite.

Old-school lowriders, called bombs or lead sleds, rode low to the ground and were decorated with extra chrome, sirens, fender skirts, and spotlights. The original lowriders put bags of sand or cement in their cars' trunks to lower the rear ends. "Torching" was another method of lowering the car, where the springs were heated until they were red-hot, making them sag and the car ride lower.

But once these cars were lowered, they stayed low. Preferable methods were ones that allowed drivers of lowriders to raise and lower their cars to avoid run-ins with the law for driving vehicles that scraped the pavement.

After World War II, there were plenty of spare parts from the aircraft industry in the junkyards of Southern California. Ron Aguirre, a California lowrider, came up with the solution to use aircraft hydraulic cylinders to raise and lower his car. Another method of raising and lowering a car's body uses air bags for each tire, and an air tank and compressor to empty and fill the bags.

Accessories make a lowrider. Exquisite upholstery, chrome, fog lights, mirrors to show off the engine, sound systems, TVs, neon underlighting, pinstriping, and airbrush paintings are all ways owners make their rides look good. Steering wheels are also important. Some of the most popular are small wheels made of chrome chain links, known as "fat man" wheels because they allow more space for a large driver's belly.

This book was written to celebrate the artistry, inventiveness, mechanical aptitude, resilience, and humor that are all part of lowrider culture.

A NOTE FROM THE ARTIST

I have been drawing for most of my life, and I love it because anyone anywhere can do it. Drawing requires the simplest tools—cavemen used sticks with burnt tips to create detailed drawings of the lives they lived, directly onto the walls of their caves!

When I was a young boy, I would spend hours dreaming up worlds using ballpoint pens on paper bags or newsprint. I didn't have "professional tools." I didn't need them. Ballpoint pens can be found just about anywhere. Sometimes I found mine on the sidewalk, or local businesses gave them away for free with their names written along the side. I still get them this way.

I decided to draw *Lowriders in Space* with red, blue, and black ballpoint pens to revisit the excitement I felt as a kid whenever I drew. Where do you get your ballpoint pens, and what kind of drawings do you like to make? —**Raúl the Third**

What Does it Mean / ¿Que significa?

These words include Mexican-American slang, car, and astronomy terms.

a tu derecha—to your right

airbrush—a way of painting that uses air to spray the paint in a fine mist onto the car

asteroid—Smaller than a planet, asteroids are made of rock, metal, and ice. Many can be found in the asteroid belt between the planets Mars and Jupiter.

¡Ay chihuahua!—nonsense expression of frustration

bajito y suavecito—low and slow (the motto of lowriders everywhere)

barrio—neighborhood

biblioteca—library

¡Caliente!—Hot!

campeones—champions

chrome—the shiny metal on bumpers, mirrors, and other metal car parts

¡Colorín Colorado!—Just as you begin a story, "Once upon a time . . . ," these are nonsense words that mean it is the end of the story.

compressors—devices that pump air from an air reservoir (a storage container) into air bags, which when filled, raise the car, and when emptied, lower the car.

cuate—buddy

cumbia—a dance from Colombia

customize—to make something just how you want it

¡Dale gas!—Give it some gas! *or* Let's go!

dinero—money

detail—to clean and keep up your car; to remove dirt and scratches to make your car shine

El Chavo Flapjack—Flapjack's nickname is a reference to the classic Mexican TV character El Chavo del Ocho, who wears the same kind of hat as Flapjack and sits in a barrel instead of a pail.

el jefe—boss

¡Encuéntrame unas piedras con chispas!—Find me some rocks with sparkles!

ese—buddy, dude, pal

¡Estellar!—Stellar! *or* Awesome!

gearshift—a lever in the floor of the car that lets the driver change the car's gears to go faster or slower

¡Gracias!—Thank you!

homes—short for "homeboy," something you call a friend or person you know.

homies—plural of homes

hubcap—metal covers for the center part of a car's wheel

impala—a fast-moving African antelope. Also, Chevrolet Impalas are one of the favorite lowrider cars.

interesante—interesting

Io—one of the planet Jupiter's moons, which is known for its volcanoes

la luna de conejo—the rabbit in the moon. (In the United States, people see a man in the moon, but Aztec culture saw a rabbit in the moon.)

¡Mi cinto!—My belt!

Milky Way—the galaxy, or group of stars, that surround the Earth and the solar system. When you look up overhead at a very dark sky, and it appears milky with stars, you are looking at the Milky Way.

miren—look

mole—thick Mexican sauce for meat, made of many ingredients, including peppers and chocolate

monstruo—monster

northern lights—colored lights that appear near the North Pole. They are often white, blue, green, or pink and appear to dance like a light show. They are caused when charged particles from the sun bump into gas particles of Earth's atmosphere. Northern lights are also called aurora borealis.

órale—all right, right on, OK, what's up?

Orion—a constellation in the northern sky shaped like a giant hunter. It's easy to spot the three stars of his belt.

pinstripe—a thin stripe that decorates a car

Pleiades—a little cluster of seven stars named after the seven daughters of Atlas (from the Greek myth), who were placed in the sky to hide from Orion. The Aztecs drew the stars as shells in their codices (the writings of their beliefs).

Pluto—Discovered in 1930, Pluto was thought to be the ninth planet in the solar system, but in 2006, it was reclassified as a dwarf planet. It was named after Pluto, the Greek god of the underworld.

¡Que chido!—Cool!

¿Que significa?—What does it mean?

¡Que suave!—How smooth! or How cool!

ranfla—lowrider

retro-nuevo—old and new

Salton Sea—a large saltwater lake in Southern California that is slowly drying up into a salty desert.

¡Ten cuidado!—Be careful! or Watch out!

tuck and roll—a method of stitching the upholstery on car seats

V-8—a powerful eight-cylinder car engine

Vacaville—a city in Northern California

¡Vámonos!—Let's go!

vato—dude, guy

vulcanized—a way of heating up rubber to make it stronger (named after the word volcano)

¡Y hay un montón de carros!—And there's a ton of cars!

¡Y vamos a tener que echarle ganas!—And we will have to give it our best!

To my family, to Matty, to Christopher Monaghan, and to Jambi—I remember you! —**Cathy Camper**

To Mama, for daily visits to the biblioteca; Dad for his stories; my two bros for playing make-believe; my wife, Elaine, for twenty years of love and adventure; and little Raulito the Fourth for being perfect. —**Raúl the Third**

ACKNOWLEDGMENTS

Thanks to: Jose Barajas, who read it FIRST!

. . . and to Matty Monaghan, Raúl Gonzalez III, Jon Scieszka, Megan McDonald, David Henry Sterry and Arielle Eckstut (The Book Doctors), Jennifer Laughran, Catherine Wynne, Ginee Seo, Taylor Norman, Neil Egan, Kevin Sampsell, Lee Montgomery, Michael Schaub, Alison Hallett, Dave Kiersh, Jo Tracy, Ana Schmitt, Delia M. Palomeque Morales, Laura Jones, Paulina Aguirre-Clinch, Rita Jimenez, Diana Nunez, Violeta Garza, Diana Miranda, Josh Rodriguez, Deborah Gitlitz, Katie O'Dell, Rob Schmieder, Ivan Velez Jr., Dylan Williams, Aron Nels Steinke, Angie Larson, Rudy Ubaldo, Byrd, Cynthia Cowen, Constance Williams, Christopher Gruener, Leonore Gordon, Myra Kooy, Karena Beuter, Rob Kirby, John Capecci, Jen Camper, VONA, Mat Johnson and my VONA graphic novel pals, Multnomah County Library staff and resources, my family, and everyone else who believed in and supported this escapade! Plus a heartfelt thank-you to *Lowrider* magazine and their car shows, Manic Hispanic, El Vez, and the magnificent Hernandez Brothers, who inspired me. —**C. C.**

Thank you to Clark Jackson for assisting me with the undercoat of the lowrider with his handy sky-blue Bic pen. —**R**

First paperback edition published in 2014 by Chronicle Books LLC.
Also available in hardcover in 2014 by Chronicle Books LLC.

Text copyright © 2014 by Cathy Camper.
Illustrations copyright © 2014 by Raúl Gonzalez.
All rights reserved. No part of this book may be reproduced in any form without written permission from the publisher.

The Library of Congress has cataloged the hardcover edition as follows:
Library of Congress Cataloging-in-Publication Data

Camper, Cathy, author.
  Lowriders in space / by Cathy Camper ; illustrated by Raul Gonzalez III.
    pages cm. — (Lowriders ; book 1)
  Spanish words and phrases used throughout English text.
  Summary: Lupe, Flapjack, Elirio customize their car into a lowrider for the Universal Car Competition to win the cash prize that will enable them to buy their own garage.
    ISBN 978-1-4521-2155-0 (alk. paper)
  1. Lowriders—Comic books, strips, etc. 2. Competition (Psychology)—Comic books, strips, etc. 3. Friendship—Comic books, strips, etc. 4. Lowriders—Juvenile fiction. 5. Competition (Psychology)—Juvenile fiction. 6. Friendship—Juvenile fiction. 7. Graphic novels. [1. Graphic novels. 2. Lowriders—Fiction.

3. Competition (Psychology)—Fiction. 4. Friendship—Fiction. 5. Mexican Americans—Fiction.] I. Gonzalez, Raul, 1976- illustrator. II. Title. III. Title: Lowriders in space.

PZ7.7.C363Lo 2014
741.5'973—dc23

2013040709

ISBN 978-1-4521-2869-6

Manufactured in China.

Design by Neil J. Egan III.
Additional typesetting by Liam Flanagan and Mia Johnson.
Typeset in Comiccraft Hedge Backwards, P22 Posada, and ITC Century.

20 19 18 17 16 15 14 13 12

Chronicle Books LLC
680 Second Street
San Francisco, California 94107

Chronicle Books—we see things differently. Become part of our community at www.chroniclekids.com.